Crabby Gabby

Written by: Stephen Cosgrove
Illustrated by: Robin James

A Serendipity™ Book

PRICE/STERN/SLOAN
Publishers

Dedicated to my friend Robert Crosby, in search of himself and all that is around him. Always Gabby but never crabby.

Stephen

Beyond the time when you fall asleep, in a place beyond your final dreams, is a land of mystical, magical melodies. A land of soft, velvet trees and giggling, wandering streams. A place where all wishes come true and nothing happens that you don't want to.

It was in this land that certain little creatures lived and saw all that could be seen. They, like always and before, were called Furry Eyefulls. They wandered from valley to valley, looking at a little bit of this and wondering at a little bit of that.

One special Furry Eyefull, smaller than the rest and more talkative than most, was Gabby. She not only wanted to see all that she could see, but had to tell everyone about it as they were seeing it too.

Day in and day out Gabby was the one who suggested what the Furry Eyefulls did for the day. She awakened everyone in the morning with her excited chatter about all the things they would do and see.

"Wake up! Wake up! It's time for a new Gabby-Game!" she shouted eagerly. "Today we must see where the river pours into the sea!" One by one, the Furries woke with a stretch and a yawn and followed Gabby to another beautiful sight.

Day by day, week by week, Gabby suggested this and suggested that in all her Gabby-Games. But soon the suggestions turned into requests and the requests turned into demands.

"Come on! Come on! I have a new Gabby-Game!" she shouted. "We must go see the parading peacocks!"

The whole gaggle of Furry Eyefulls rushed to see the peacocks. They settled into the gentle meadow moss and prepared to watch for hours and hours. Then, as the peacocks fanned their gorgeous tails, Gabby was rushing them off to somewhere else.

"Hurry! Hurry! We must get to the lake in the woods to watch the silver fish flash in the noontime sun!" she demanded. And off the Furry Eyefulls went, waddling through the woods.

After they had sat by the lake for a time or two, Gabby jumped to her fuzzy feet and said, dusting the leaves from her fur, "Well, that's enough of that. Now we are all going deep into the forest and throw nuts and pine cones at the chipmunks. It's one of my most favorite Gabby-Games. Come on guys, let's go!" And with that, they all stood and started to leave.

But one of the younger Furry Eyefulls spoke up, "I really don't want to play another Gabby-Game. Why don't we all just sit awhile and watch the fish in the lake?"

Well, Gabby was fit to be tied. "Why don't *you* just sit there, then?" she asked sacrastically. "In fact why don't you play a new Gabby-Game with your friends, the fish?" Then she booted the little furry creature into the lake. The other Furry Eyefulls laughed and laughed as the younger one tried to climb from the water with a lilypad on his head. Then they followed Gabby down the trail.

The Eyefulls waddled to the middle of the forest to the tall, stately hazel tree where all the chipmunks lived. Gabby picked up a pine cone and threw it, narrowly missing a tiny chipmunk who scampered out of the way. Then all the Furries started throwing hazel nuts and sticks at the other chipmunks chattering angrily in the branches.

Gabby just laughed and laughed to see the chipmunks dodging this way and that. Copying Gabby, all the other Furry Eyefulls joined in her giggling and laughter. It seemed like such a good Gabby-Game.

Finally one of the Furries said, "Hey, maybe we shouldn't be doing this. After all, the poor little chipmunks have a right to be in the forest, too!"

Gabby looked at her in disbelief. "Oh, you like the little chipmunks, huh? Well, if you like the chipmunks so much you can have all their nuts!" And with that, she threw the nuts in the other Furry's face. The other little Eyefulls did the same, and ran after Gabby, leaving the poor little creature all alone.

Later that very same day Gabby led everyone into the meadow to play a game with her ball. "Hurry! Hurry!" she yelled. "We're going to play a brand-new Gabby-Game."

"What is a Gabby-Game?" one of them asked.

Gabby quickly answered, "Silly, a Gabby-Game is a game where Gabby makes up all the rules and everybody has to play."

"Well, that doesn't seem very fair," another little Furry said.

"Well," said Gabby, "you don't have to play, but it is my ball. So, it's a Gabby-Game or nothing."

All but the one Furry Eyefull decided to play, looking to Gabby for the rules of the brand-new Gabby-Game.

So, she explained the simple rules of her Gabby-Game. "First everyone throws the ball to me and then I throw the ball to someone else. The winner is the one who catches the ball the most."

"Wait a minute," said one of the Eyefulls. "If we always have to throw the ball back to you then you will always win!"

"Of course," said Gabby gleefully. "After all, it's my ball and this is a Gabby-Game!"

All the other Eyefulls looked at one another and then back at Gabby, who was throwing the ball idly from one hand to the other.

"You know," said the Eyefulls, "we have gone from pond to stream to see and do only those things that you wanted to see and do. We don't want to play your Gabby-Games anymore!" Then they all walked away, leaving Gabby alone in the meadow with her favorite ball and her only friend . . . herself.

"Pooh! What do they know? They'll find that without me there isn't any fun. I'll just wait and see." With the ball as a pillow, she stretched in the cool grasses of the meadow, waiting for the other Furry Eyefulls to return.

She waited and waited and finally fell asleep, dreaming selfish dreams of always winning at her Gabby-Games. When she woke she found that she was still alone. The other Furry Eyefulls had not come back. "Fools!" she thought. "Well, I'll show them who's the boss!" Gabby set off in search of her friends through the forest of ferns. She searched and searched, until she finally found them sitting and staring at all the beautiful blooming flowers in a tiny, tiny meadow.

"Well, it's time for a new Gabby-Game!" Gabby announced. "Come on, we are all going to go throw nuts at the chipmunks again! Let's go!" She raced back through the forest to the tree where the chipmunks lived, but when she got there she found that she was all alone. Nobody wanted to play her Gabby-Games anymore.

With a thump, she sat on an old rotted stump and began to cry and cry. Over her crying she could hear the soft, gentle slithering of Kartusch, a kindly, blind snake who lived in the forest. "Why do you cry, little one?" asked the snake in a quiet hiss.

"None of the other Furry Eyefulls want to play my Gabby-Games anymore." Then, in a halting voice, she told Kartusch of all that had happened.

Kartusch wrapped himself around a sun-warmed rock and thought for a moment. "Gabby," he said, "things are to be seen and games are to be played — not just to win but for the enjoyment of the game or the pleasure in the things that you look at. The other Furry Eyefulls don't want to play anymore because you always have to win. When you are ready to play and to see those things around you for the enjoyment of them rather than the victory, you will always win even though you may lose the game."

Gabby's tears slowly dried in the warmth of Kartusch's words, and she knew that he was right.

Day after day thereafter, Gabby learned to play with the other Furry Eyefulls. She learned to win in losing, and under the watchful eye of a kindly, blind snake called Kartusch, she never played her Gabby-Games again.

WHEN YOU LEAD AND
WHEN YOU PLAY
YOUR SELFISH GABBY-GAMES
REMEMBER IT'S NOT JUST WINNING
THAT MAKES THE GAME A GAME

Serendipity™ Books

Written by Stephen Cosgrove
Illustrated by Robin James

Enjoy all the delightful books in the Serendipity series:

($1.95 each)
*also available with cassette ($4.95)

For a free list of P/S/S titles, send your name and address along with a self-addressed, stamped envelope.

The above titles are available wherever books are sold, or can be ordered directly from the publisher. Send your check or money order for the total amount plus $1.00 for handling and mailing to:

DIRECT MAIL SALES

PRICE/STERN/SLOAN *Publishers, Inc.*
410 North La Cienega Boulevard, Los Angeles, California 90048

Prices slightly higher in Canada